DATE DUE

APR 1 1994			
MAY 4 1992			

a division of The All Children's Company, Ltd., 1991
First American edition, 1991

Library of Congress catalog card number: 90–28860

Published simultaneously in Canada by HarperCollinsCanadaLtd

Printed in Hong Kong

To my own aunts and uncles

who gave me the taste for adventure

JH

For Lucy

PU

Text copyright © 1991 by Judy Hindley
Illustrations copyright © 1991 by Peter Utton

All rights reserved

First published in Great Britain by ABC, All Books for Children,
a division of The All Children's Company, Ltd, 1991
First American edition, 1991

Library of Congress catalog card number: 90–28860

Published simultaneously in Canada by HarperCollins*Canada Ltd*

Printed in Hong Kong

Uncle Harold and the Green Hat

written by

JUDY HINDLEY

illustrated by

PETER UTTON

Farrar, Straus and Giroux
New York

My Uncle Harold is solid and square.
He has an astonishing up-and-down chair,
and a sink with a fountain
and mirrors and cranes
that could make such amazing construction machines —
though my Uncle Harold (BSc, DDS)
seems hardly ever to notice those things.

But he never plays,
no, nothing like that.
Not till the day
when he found the Green Hat.
He looked oddly unsettled
that day when I found him,
marooned in his room with his instruments round him —
he seemed baffled and scared,
and he gazed, as he sat,
at an object that strongly resembled a hat;
but how could a hat
(be it ever so bright)
require his nostrils to quiver with fright?

"Oh, Malcolm!" he begged me.
"Don't do what I did!
That hat is a patient's!
I know I was wrong.
Whatever you do, Malcolm —
DON'T PUT IT ON!"

But of course, with each word
the allure of it grew.
I couldn't resist it!
Well, really — could you?

"No!" cried my uncle.
"No –" he cried. "Wait!"
"No, DON'T!" he implored me –

But it was too late.

What luck that my uncle
took my arm, at this point,
though he almost completely
uncoupled the joint;
for as quick as a flash,
with a CRASH! and a roar
we were zooped by the head
through a gap in the door.
"Malcolm, my boy!"
he beseeched, as we sped.
"When you put on the hat –
WHAT WENT ON IN YOUR HEAD?

"I told you! I warned you!
Now, Malcolm – be serious!"

But a new thought had struck me,
and I was delirious.
"Oh, Uncle!" I cried.
"This is great! It's so neat!
We could think ourselves
lifetime provisions of SWEETS!"

All too quickly it happened –
a rumbling like thunder –
and goodies came tumbling
till we were snowed under!

Gumdrops and gobstoppers,
pastries and pies,
chocolates and toffees,
right up to our eyes.

Caramels! Cream puffs!
Cakes and ice-cream.
Well – it rained and snowed sweets
till I thought I would scream!

"Just like an avalanche
high in the Alps!"
I thoughtlessly thought,
risking both of our scalps,
for of course (as I'm sure
you all perfectly know)
if I THOUGHT snow
we GOT snow.
And BLOOP!
It was so.

"Faster!" I heard my poor relative plead.
"Quick, Malcolm! Save us. Think quickly!
Think SPEED!"

Oh, he shouldn't have said it!
For what could I do?
I thought of the speediest thing that I knew.

Sure enough, we were soon whizzing up in a rocket.
"Malcolm!" I heard.
"Now you've just got to STOP IT!"

"But how?" I entreated,
and I heard him call.
"DON'T THINK!"
cried my uncle.
"Just DON'T THINK AT ALL!"

I tried to stop thinking.
I tried fit to burst.
At last, I thought
    NOTHING
and that was the worst.

"Think again!" came the order.
I heard myself groan.
For now all I wanted and wished for
was HOME.

Well, would you believe it?
That's all it took,
and
    WHOOOOOSH!
we were back there
in Uncle's small nook.

And there in the corner
quite calmly he sat —
the little green man
who belonged to the hat.

"Ah, my hat," he said simply.
"I think – do you mind? –
I may just have possibly
left it behind?"

"But of course," said my uncle.
"Do take it. Please do.
We're ever so sorry –
such a bother for you.

"But when were you here?
Was I in when you came?
I don't think I saw you —"
"Few do," said the man.
"Oh, INDEED," said my uncle.
He said it with feeling,
for the leprechaun vanished —
straight through the ceiling.

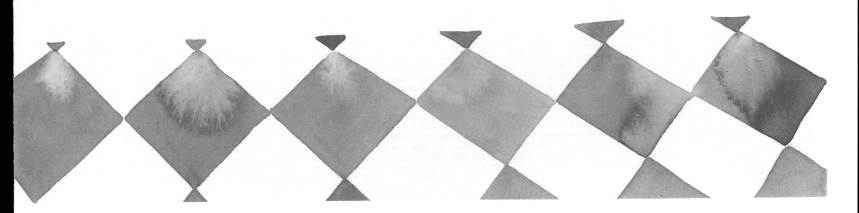

My uncle, I saw, was sincerely relieved
when the miniature stranger
at last took his leave . . .
"Well, that's that," said my uncle.
"A dear little fellow.
– But who can have left this
PURPLE UMBRELLA?"